For Jade. D.S.
To Lin. G.B.

American edition published in 2014 by Andersen Press USA,
an imprint of Andersen Press Ltd.
www.andersenpressusa.com
First published in Great Britain in 2014 by Andersen Press Ltd.,
20 Vauxhall Bridge Road, London SW1V 2SA.
Published in Australia by Random House Australia Pty.,
Level 3, 100 Pacific Highway, North Sydney, NSW 2060.
Text copyright © Dyan Sheldon, 2014.
Illustration copyright © Gary Blythe, 2014.

Distributed in the United States and Canada by
Lerner Publishing Group, Inc.
241 First Avenue North
Minneapolis, MN 55401 USA
For reading levels and more information, look up this title at www.lernerbooks.com.

Color separated in Switzerland by Photolitho AG, Zürich.
Printed and bound in Malaysia by Tien Wah Press.
Gary Blythe has used acrylic on board in this book.

Library of Congress Cataloging-in-Publication data available.
ISBN: 978-1-4677-6314-1
eBook ISBN: 978-1-4677-6318-9
1 – TWP – 4/15/14

The Moon Dragons

DYAN SHELDON
GARY BLYTHE

ANDERSEN PRESS USA

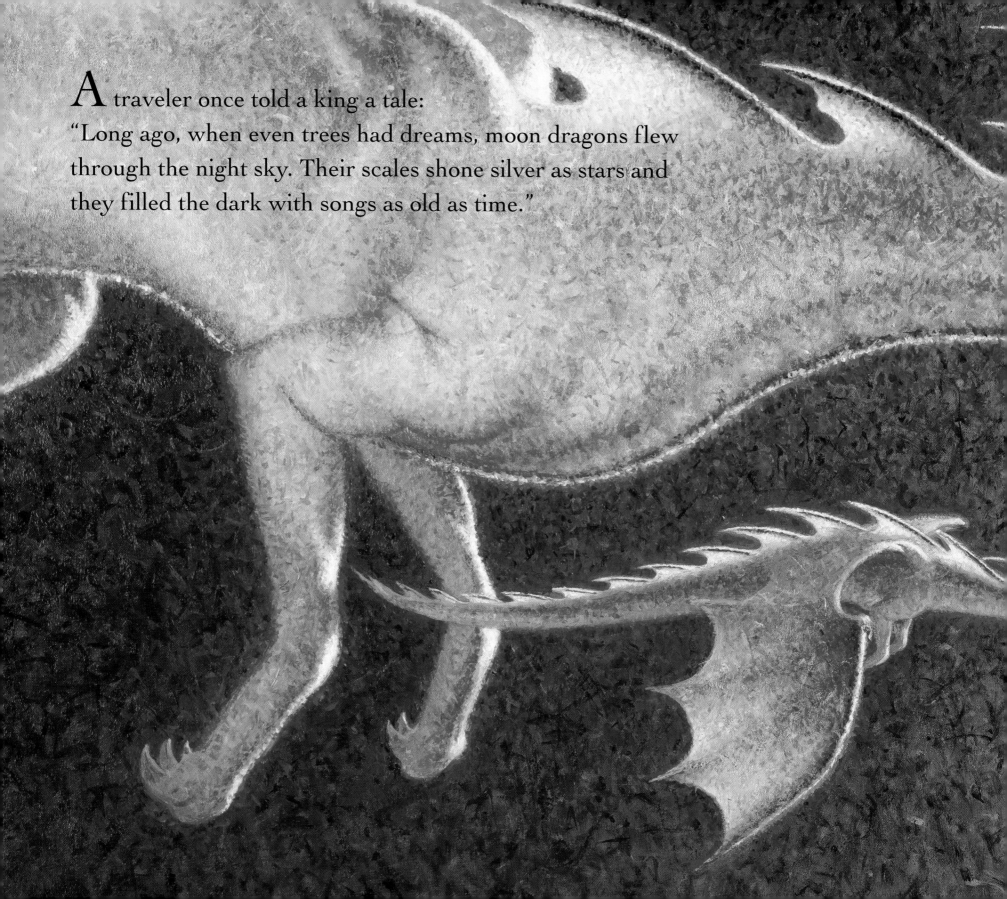

A traveler once told a king a tale:
"Long ago, when even trees had dreams, moon dragons flew
through the night sky. Their scales shone silver as stars and
they filled the dark with songs as old as time."

"I know all about them," snapped the king. "But what use are they to me with their silver scales and singing? They've all been killed."

"Not all of them." The traveler pointed to a distant mountaintop, poking through the clouds. "A few survived. They hide up there."

After the traveler left, the king summoned the royal huntsmen.
"I want a moon dragon!" he commanded. "Go up that mountain and bring one back!"
"But, Sire–" the huntsmen protested.
"Now!" ordered the king.

The royal huntsmen went up the mountain.
But its slopes were steep and treacherous,
its woods filled with frightening beasts.

When they returned, all they had was a goat.

"Did I ask for a *goat*?" The king's voice rose. "No, I did not! I asked for a dragon!"

"We didn't see any dragons," said the royal huntsmen.

"I don't care what you saw!" roared the king. "I am king! I get whatever I want! Send messengers to every corner of the kingdom. I'll give a room full of gold to whoever finds the moon dragons."

The messengers were sent. Men came from all over – hunters, trappers and adventurers; woodsmen, herders and mountaineers – each of them after the room full of gold. But none of them found so much as a silver scale.

The last person to hear about the quest was Alina. She lived alone at the foot of the mountain. Her grandmother used to tell her stories about the moon dragons, their beauty and their mystery.
Sometimes they sailed through Alina's dreams.
"I'm going to find them," said Alina.

The villagers laughed. "You're not a hunter or a trapper or an adventurer," they shouted. "You're just a poor girl who gathers firewood and berries." The king and his court laughed too.
"You're not a woodsman or a herdsman or a mountaineer," howled the king. "You're just a child."
"I'm still going to find the moon dragons," said Alina.

Everyone might laugh, but Alina knew the mountain and its forests as well as any goat or deer. Up she went, singing a song that her grandmother had taught her. She was thinking not of the room full of gold, but of a time when even trees had dreams.

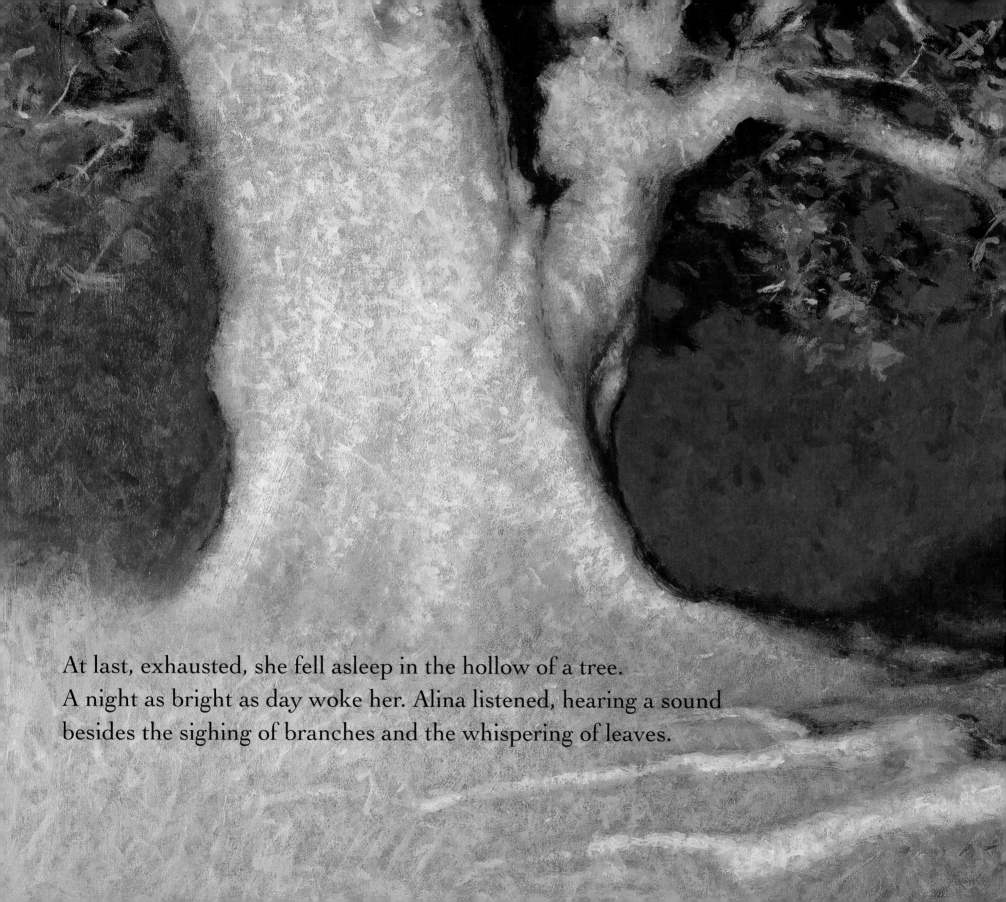

At last, exhausted, she fell asleep in the hollow of a tree.
A night as bright as day woke her. Alina listened, hearing a sound
besides the sighing of branches and the whispering of leaves.

Slowly and quietly, Alina followed the sound to the top of a hill.
And there, in the dale below, was a dance of dragons, shining pearl and silver in the soft lunar light.

As Alina watched, first one then another rose into the air, graceful as clouds, their voices joined in song.

Alina stood on the hilltop as if in a dream. Her heart beat with the singing of the dragons, her breath flowed with the rhythm of their wings.

"Did you find the dragons?" the villagers asked when she returned. Alina stared back at their eager faces. She knew the king would put the dragons in cages or kill them and hang their heads on the palace walls.

"No," said Alina. "I didn't find them. Not a trace."

"Didn't we tell you?" scoffed the villagers.

Their laughter followed her all the way home.

But as she walked along, Alina took a silver scale from her pocket and smiled. A flight of dragons was worth far more than a room full of gold.